About the Author

Beverley is a radio host and vlogger based in Meath, Ireland. She has a background in Marketing. In her spare time, she enjoys food, fitness and fashion designing.

Ernest and The Prince of Peace

Beverley Joseph

Ernest and The Prince of Peace

Olympia Publishers
London

www.olympiapublishers.com
OLYMPIA PAPERBACK EDITION

A CIP catalogue record for this title is available from the British Library.

ISBN: 978-1-78830-512-9

First Published in 2020

Olympia Publishers
Tallis House
2 Tallis Street
London
EC4Y 0AB
Printed in Great Britain

Dedication

For my Jesus, the real Prince of Peace.

Acknowledgements

I'd like to thank my wonderful mum & dad for always loving and supporting me.

My little cousins, Eli and Elic for prodding me to tell them stories until I came up with this creation.

Finally, I'd like to thank Olympia Publishers and James Houghton for believing in my work.

Once upon a time in a beautiful far away land lived a charming and handsome young prince called, Ernest. Ernest was a boy of many gifts and talents, he could lift three hundred logs all at once, he ran cross-country, but most of all his heart was full of love. He took his official duties very seriously. He visited the noble folk, helped look after his little brother, Lesley, and was always ready to help anyone around the Kingdom. But sometimes being a crown prince was a hard job for such a young boy, especially when his parents went away on royal duties.

What made things even harder for Ernest was a family secret, a secret about him that he had to carry around all the time. Sometimes it made him feel sad, at other times it made him feel scared. The secret was that his ears were too big, so big that he had to hide them under his hair or a hat.

One day at a royal function, Ernest's friend, Victor, was in a naughty mood. He thought it would be a funny idea to pull Ernest's hat off. But Victor didn't know that Ernest had just had a fresh haircut from the royal barber that day!

As Victor pulled off Ernest's hat everyone saw Ernest's big ears!

Suddenly everyone became silent. Not even a mouse was heard moving.

The people sighed in amazement.

Then a little boy in the crowd began to giggle. "Look at Prince Ernest's big ears!" he said as he pointed at them.

The whole crowd began to laugh.

Ernest's face turned bright red. First, he was shocked. Then he felt hurt. He ran off the royal stage as his eyes began to fill up with tears. It seemed like the whole kingdom knew Ernest's big secret! They laughed at him. Ernest was scared that people may think he is not a good prince. Ernest was worried that people would not like him anymore because his ears were unusual.

As Ernest lay awake that night, he thought about how he could fix his ears. 'If only I could find a way to make my ears normal like everyone else's!' he wished.

Then he remembered someone the bad folks from other kingdoms went to see when they needed a 'quick fix,' The Wicked Witch of Sholah. She lived in a desolate cave a little far away. Ernest knew that the king and queen didn't like her. After all, she was a wicked witch. But he wanted things to become better so much that he ignored what he knew was right, hoping that she would make things better.

So that night, when everyone in the castle had fallen asleep, Ernest snuck out of his window and tiptoed quietly passed the guard who was busy tying up his shoelace.

Ernest untied his pet horse, Chumley, from the stable and headed eastward to Sholah.

He finally arrived at the cave.

Ernest left Chumley outside and peered in through the cave. He heard a strange cackling laugh. It must be the wicked witch! He followed the noise into the cave.

Soon he saw her. The most frightening figure he had ever seen. She looked up at him with beady eyes and a large crooked nose. "So, Prince Ernest... I finally meet you today! I've been expecting you. I know all about what happened today. After all, everyone does!" She cackled.

Ernest felt scared, though he felt scared by the ugly sight of the wicked witch, he felt more scared by what she told him. "Does everyone really know?" He worried.

"Of course they do!" the wicked witch replied. "Everyone is talking about it and everyone is laughing at you!"

However, this was not the truth. Though some of the townspeople who were at the function had laughed at Prince Ernest's ears, everyone in town still hadn't heard about what happened and not everyone was talking about it. But the wicked witch had a way of lying and twisting the truth that would often lead people to make bad choices.

"Wicked Witch, can you make my ears normal like everyone else's?" Ernest asked.

"Yes, I can!" she replied. "But everything I do comes at a price!"

"What will be the price of this?" Ernest questioned.

The wicked witch looked at Prince Ernest with an evil smirk.

"I've saved up my pocket money from the last three years. I can give you–" Ernest tried to make a deal with the witch.

"Oh no, Prince Ernest!" the wicked witch cackled. "I want something far more precious than that!"

"And what is that?" Ernest questioned.

"The kingdom's amulet. The one that holds the power of all the kingdom."

The amulet was a powerful Jewel that had been kept locked away in the castle for centuries. Only the king had the key to it. This would be given to Prince Ernest when he became king, but the king had entrusted Prince Ernest with the knowledge of where it was kept. The amulet was very special and that is why it was very important. Under the right care and its rightful place in the castle.

The next day, Ernest snuck out again after it fell dark and everyone in the castle had fallen asleep. Ernest felt very nervous. He had secretly taken the amulet out of its special place and he now had it in his pocket. He felt an unhappy feeling in the pit of his stomach, something told him this wasn't the right thing to do, but his desire to be great felt stronger than his desire to do what he knew was right.

He arrived at the cave of The Wicked Witch of Sholah. It's not too late, I can still turn back and head for the castle. Ernest thought for a moment.

"Prince Ernest! Do come in, you are about to have your problem fixed." the wicked witch shouted from inside.

Ernest's thoughts were distracted by the witch's loud call. Oh… yes… my problem… my ears… the townspeople! Ernest remembered and he handed over the amulet to the wicked witch.

Ernest felt a strange tingling on his ears as they began to shrink. Ernest touched his ears to find they had become smaller.

"All done Prince Ernest, I believe our deal has been made!" The wicked witch snickered as she held on to the amulet tightly.

Ernest headed back to the castle. He was very excited. He couldn't wait to show his friends his new ears. Most of all, he was glad that he no longer had to worry about anyone making fun of him or laughing at him. But as Ernest and Chumley rode back it began to rain. Just a little at first, Ernest thought it would soon stop. But then the winds grew stronger, there was thunder and lightning and the rain became very heavy. Oh no, it was a storm! It could take a long time until Chumley and Ernest reached back to the castle. They would have to pull over for shelter and make stops along the way. Chumley would not be able to run as fast on the slippery rocks because of the rain. It was too dangerous. Ernest knew that his parents, the king and queen would be worried.

It was now the next day and when Ernest would not show up at breakfast, they would know something was wrong. After all, it wasn't like Ernest to ever miss a meal.

One day turned into two days, but Ernest and Chumley still hadn't made it home. The journey was very slow and the winds blew very hard.

Finally, on the third day, Ernest and Chumley could see the Kingdom in the horizon. They were almost there. But something looked strangely different. They could hear a battle cry coming from afar, there were flames and smoke around the kingdom.

As they got closer to the castle, they could see the king's men fighting, other kingdoms were trying to attack and their kingdom had gone to war.

Ernest's excitement soon turned into fear and worry. Is this all my fault? He wondered. Is this happening because I gave the amulet into the wrong hands? Now Ernest not only faced two very cross parents, but a very troubled Kingdom!

As Ernest entered the castle he found everyone rushing about in panic. As he made his way up the stairs and to the king and queen's throne room, he knew he was in trouble.

"Son, what have you done?" the king asked Ernest.

Ernest took a deep breath and thought about what to say.

"Son, we know it was you. Only you and your father know where the key to the place of the amulet is kept. It was missing and so were you. Where have you taken it?" the queen asked.

"I gave it to The Wicked Witch of Sholah. Look, she fixed my ears." Ernest showed them.

But the king and queen were not pleased at all, instead they looked very sad and disappointed. They had loved Ernest just the same even when his ears were big, it didn't make any difference to them whether his ears were big or small.

Ernest felt very sorry, he soon understood that in his hurry to fix things by himself he had made a very bad choice that had put the entire kingdom at harm. "I'm so sorry Mother and Father!" Ernest exclaimed. "What will happen to the kingdom now?" He asked in fear.

"We must prepare for battle!" The king told Ernest. "We have managed to defeat the other kingdoms that have come against us but the evil Kingdom of Sholah is our biggest threat. The wicked witch is helping The Prince of Darkness fight against us. Even though you are just a boy, Ernest, our defenses are low and you will also have to fight with the armies to save our kingdom." said the king.

Ernest had not been in battle before; he was too young. He knew that this meant that the kingdom was in great danger and everyone would have to do their part to save it.

As Ernest prepared to fight that evening, he felt overwhelmed by the big task in front of him. Ernest was a strong prince, but he was still a boy. He wasn't as strong as the king's best knights. He needed something to make him stronger, he needed something to give him hope and courage. He had already seen the harm and danger that came from finding quick fixes in the wrong places.

So this time he searched for true hope. He desperately rummaged around his bedroom for something he could find. He looked through all of the cupboards. He looked under his bed. But all he found were bats and balls, and old fair tickets from times he had enjoyed with his friends. Until he came to a dusty old chest in the corner of his wardrobe.

Ernest opened the chest to find a shimmering, double-edged sword inside with a letter that was given to him by his old trusted friend, The Prince of Peace. Ernest had forgotten all about the gift he had been given some time ago. He remembered how excited he had been when he first received the gift by The Prince of Peace. He wanted to be just like him. Brave and strong, wise and kind. He had read the letter more times than he could remember. It had told Ernest how to be strong and wise.

How could he have forgotten? He wondered. If only he had remembered all that The Prince of Peace had told him in the letter, he would never have given the amulet into the wrong hands.

Ernest knew that by remembering the good advice of his trusted friend, The Prince of Peace, he could help restore the peace of the kingdom. He would use the sharp and strong double-edged sword to fight off the evil powers of Sholah's armies.

Ernest entered the battle ground with his father, the king, his most noble knights and the kingdom's army. It was a dangerous and scary time. There was a lot of noise and the giant horses coming against Ernest and Chumley seemed no match for them. But Ernest knew he had to be brave and the wise words of The Prince of Peace filled his heart with courage.

That day Ernest fought his hardest as Chumley ran his fastest. Suddenly they heard a loud squeal behind them.

"Run Son, run!" Ernest heard the King shout to him.

But as Ernest tugged on Chumley's reigns to go, he realised it was too late. He had come face to face with Sholah's strongest fighter, the hideous two-headed monster, Leviathan. Ernest looked on in horror as Leviathan opened his two mouths. He was coming fast towards Ernest with his sharp fangs. Ernest grabbed onto the double-edged sword and struck Leviathan with all his might.

Leviathan fell down with a loud crash as the double-edged sword sliced through his two heads. And so the evil Kingdom of Sholah was defeated. As the good news reached the castle, the queen and all of the townspeople rejoiced! According to the old laws of the land, the wicked witch was forced to switch back the deal she had made with Ernest. Since Sholah had been defeated it would have to return the amulet back. But this also meant that Ernest's ears would return to the way they had been before the deal was made.

Ernest was very excited to hear that his great friend, The Prince of Peace, would join him and his father, the king, on their journey to get back the amulet. When they arrived at the cave Ernest saw how terrified the Wicked Witch of Sholah was by the powerful light of The Prince of Peace. Light and goodness were The Prince of Peace's special powers and no evil could stand them, not even the wicked witch.

As the wicked witch handed back the amulet to Ernest his ears began to tingle again and returned back to their regular size.

As Ernest, The Prince of Peace and the king rode back towards the kingdom, Ernest began to wonder how the kingdom would act towards him now that his ears were big again.

"Do you think they will make fun of me?" Ernest asked The Prince of Peace.

"What matters most Ernest is what you know to be true about yourself, not what others think of you. When you understand this, you will be happy being just the way you are instead of trying to be like everyone else."

Ernest knew that these words of The Prince of Peace were very important and that he must remember them in order to be a good prince. That day, Ernest realised that a good prince is strong enough to stand apart to do the right thing even when everyone else is joining in to do the wrong thing. A good prince is happier doing the right thing, even if it may mean being made fun of.

Ernest is a young, kind and courageous prince, but an unusual family secret keeps him from living life to the full. He lives life constantly watching his back, faced with the danger of others finding out about it. Ernest is left with an important decision to make. His exciting story is jam packed with the adventure, mystery and action that every little boy dreams of. Ernest faces the challenge of choosing good from evil, learning what really matters and whom to trust. Will it be a happy ending for Ernest? Find out.

Olympia Publishers   **Children's fiction**

ISBN   978-1-78830-512-9

9 781788 305129

Author: **Beverley Joseph**

£5.99   €8.99

www.olympiapublishers.com